The Book of Christmas Tales

Jake Palmer

To

Warner.

Jake Palmer
x

Also by Jake Palmer

THE JOURNEY TO THE SHORE AND

OTHER SUMMER TALES

Acknowledgements:

To those who encouraged me to write my debut

earlier in the year. Have a great Christmas and

New Year!

Contents

Tale 1:

A Christmas Surprise

James had lived in a small flat in a tall concrete building with his Mum and his annoying younger sister but was under the strict rule of a very evil landlord called Mr. Cooke. Landlords these days are often kind, born with a very affectionate heart and soul; but this one was a monster! A rogue, who would not have pets living in the flats, that upset James often.

At school one day, as it was a very bleak early December morning, as the term was about to end for Christmas, his teacher Miss Appleyear, asked the class to write a letter to Father Christmas, to see what they would like in time for Christmas Day.

"Now as you write your letter to Santa," Miss Appleyear announced, "you must think about what you want and will have the rest of this lesson to complete it." She pulled up a pen and wrote some sentences on the whiteboard to help the others and James write their letters to Santa, and after some guidance, a timer was set and the classroom was full of silence.

This girl, called Ava-Mae, sat next to him and whispered: "I can't believe that evil landlord won't let you have a puppy!" He and Ava-Mae were proper best friends, and even though they could argue about the little pathetic things like normal friends would do, they'd make up and be happy like they did before.

Later that evening, as he, his Mum and his three-year-old sister Valerie, who was very noisy and naughty by the way, sat at the dining table that was in the kitchen eating spaghetti and meatballs, James had something to say which made his Mum wonder. "What do you have to say, sweetheart? You can tell me anything, you know that, don't you?"

"Mum," James had replied, deftly turning a little angle towards his who sat next to him. "Can I have a puppy for Christmas? Just like Theo."

Theo, one of his favorite plush toy bears, had been with James since he was first a baby, and up to now had been James' best friend, along with his panda plush bear Winslow, who looked quite mischievous by the slant on his face, had grey and white fur, and a scarf with glitter and shine beautifully when it came into contact with the light, which at during day and night it was on, with no reason at all.

"You know you can't," his Mum had to disappoint him with a reminder, "otherwise that crabby, devilish old goat would catch us and throw us out."

Morally, he felt like his dreams had just been crushed by decline and rejection and started to burst out crying, full-on tears coming out of his hazel eyes, rushing to his bedroom and the door slammed, making the ancient brick walls shake. The set of apartments had been there for a few decades, and before Mr Cooke became the landlord, there was an old woman called Mrs. Marsh who ran it and would let dogs and other animals live there, but when she sadly died a year after James, his Mum and very annoying sister (as ever) had moved in.

"Mummy," Valerie said, letting out a cough that was hoarse and rough, which often gave her chest infections, "can I have pudding now?"

"Yes, Valerie!" the Mum answered, giving Valerie a normal smile, "what do you want? A bowl of strawberry *Angel Delight* or a yummy-tummy slice of cheesecake?"

Valerie sat in her high chair, thinking very hard whilst continuously banging a spoon onto the yellow tray.

"I would like some *Angel Delight!*"

Their mum went into the kitchen, opened the fridge and got some milk and poured some into a jug and put it back. She opened the cupboard to a ninety-degree angle, got the packet of *Angel Delight* and poured the powder, which gives the colour a very rich one, to be frank!

Within five minutes, all of the *Angel Delight* was mixed up and when James was still crying in his room, firmly hugging, there was a tender tap on the door.

"Go away!" he cried, as he sobbed, using Theo as a tissue. Eww!

"I have made *Angel Delight*, please come out," his Mum said, going back to the kitchen so she could put some of it in Valerie's bowl, which was plastic. Finally, at last, James had stopped crying and walked to the kitchen, got his dish of *Angel Delight* and sat at the table to eat it.

He finished it sometime later, and some days later, Christmas break had now started and school was over until after New Year, and on the night after breaking off, James, Valerie and his Mum got onto the bus and went to the theatre to see a Christmas children's show. The show was *The Polar Express*, and it went on for an hour or two, before going home, sitting on the sofa drinking hot chocolate near the flames of that warm fire. On Christmas morning, as the turtle doves flew, spreading their snowy-white wings, it was very cold and snow had already fallen.

"Wake up, James!" Valerie cried, dashing into his room. "It's Christmas morning, Mummy's downstairs waiting for us."

"Yes!" he cheered, jumping out of bed, sprinting down the carpeted stairs, "let's open some gifts delivered by Father Christmas."

They both went into the living room and started opening their presents, but whilst they opened their presents, their Mum came through and put a well-wrapped box next to James. He stopped opening the other presents and untied the shiny red bow and the box, once tearing up the paper, opened the box and it was a puppy. A puppy that looked exactly like Theo! It was truly a surprise and the landlord got replaced by a much polite person and pets could live there again.

Tale 2:

The Letter on Christmas Eve

It was not long until Christmas. Only a few weeks, that was all. Now almost every day, almost everyone would find themselves in the shopping center getting presents for their children, sisters, brothers, parents and grandparents, so they would be sorted and wrapped and sent all ready for Christmas. Everybody was excited, even little Jack; who wanted to be a postman when he was older.

Jack Dubbin's had shiny ginger hair, light freckles on either side of his cheeks which were normally bright red, and wore round glasses that had the shape of a wide O, which at second glance, didn't have the shape of a wide O.

"Come on, Jack!" Mum said, repeatedly tapping the glass of her watch, "we don't want to be late for school."

He dashed down the stairs and his Mum held out his bag in her hands, but it was fairly heavy and wondered if he had got in there. A big whiny panda? A computer with extra accessories? She was curious, but however she didn't have time to think as she locked the house with her key and walked him to school.

"Can I meet Mason?" he asked, giving the puppy-face, which he always got away with, who couldn't get declined, not by his mum, nor anyone, "he is over there, talking to Chris."

His mum kissed him and let him go to Mason and Chris, who were his two best friends since they were adorable little babies.

Mason Hunter had brown hair, and was hilarious – especially when he told jokes that were silly and a bit cheeky; and had specs that were round and possibly made from a red sort of wood, but couldn't think what it was, and called it: "*Red Wood Round Glasses*". He wore a red jumper, a white shirt underneath, all perfectly ironed and a pair of black shoes that could have been leather and were vastly shiny, like a newly-bought car.

"Hi, Mason!" Jack cried out, waving his Mum goodbye. "Not long until the Christmas holidays now."

"I know," he replied, "have you both written your list for what you want to ask Santa?"

Both Chris and Jack nodded, and the bell rang. It was time to go to school and the December wind now became more crisp as Jack's mum walked out of the front gates of the school and went home.

"It is the last day and we are going to watch a film!" Jack's teacher Mr Williams had said, who was normally silly and hilarious, before letting off a ballerina dance, which made everybody laugh, even Jack!

The film was *Arthur Christmas* and even had popcorn. It had seemed a memorable time, a time that they would not forget ever, even when they have the quiet Miss Leonard next year. The popcorn was warm, and had just been done in the microwave and some people had thought it was hot, but it wasn't, as it seemed that they were very dramatic about it.

Later on as the Christmas break had now begun and school was now over until January, everybody could rejoice themselves with rest and enjoy their break and at the dinner table, when it was time to have tea, Jack said: "When will Santa come? What time is it when it is Christmas Eve?"

"It depends if you are asleep or not otherwise he would be able to tell, wouldn't he?" Jack's mum replied, giving him some thought about what that phrase could mean.

On Christmas Eve night where the streets were now silent and tender, and as all the children and adults were asleep, excited to unwrap their presents the next morning, a bright glow had shone into Jack's room that woke him up. Suddenly, out of nowhere, a tall and chubby man with a fluffy white beard, all dressed in red, wearing a brownish belt, came through the window and gave Jack a letter, perfectly dry from the light rain that had now started to drop down.

"Merry Christmas, Jack!" the man said, only realizing it was Santa, "and a Happy New Year, ho-ho-ho."

It was the best Christmas yet.

Tale 3:

The Story of Emily Kingfisher

The tale that I am going to tell you is the tale that includes a jovial kingfisher, who loved the season of winter and Christmas, and her fur was more silken than a Japanese Maple tree. This kingfisher wasn't one of those normal ones that you would see normally, but this kingfisher was known as a "Christmas Kingfisher", and they are very hard to find.

Why are they called *Christmas Kingfishers*? Well, the reason they are called Christmas Kingfishers is because they have snowy-white fur, rich ocean-blue eyes and their feathers are light as a baby spider. Also they are called this because birdwatchers are obsessed with them and never saw this type of wonderful bird; and had questions saying in his head: "How come I haven't seen this beautiful creature before?" and the reason is that there weren't many of the *Christmas Kingfishers* left.

One morning, as the bitter coldness had settled into the vast valley where monkeys, parrots, red pandas and birds lived, shortly after the sun rose into the somber grey sky, Emily woke up from her night sleep and flew to the tall bird bath, where magnificently the water had not become frozen yet.

"A very nice morning!" she said to herself, adding with a tenderly tweet, "even if it is December, it is still cold."

She hopped into the bath, and at that exact moment when she touched the biting, icy water, her feathers shook violently, shaking because of the coldness of the shallow water.

Another kingfisher came and went in the bath too, and yes! – it was her friend Piper, who was a year younger than Emily. "Hi, Emily!"

Emily tweeted, as her teeth clattered into each other time and time again. Her teeth kept on clattering because during the winter, once all of the coldness had settled into the valley, her teeth would clatter so much that her delicate mouth would swell up, and caused pain which made her cry sometimes.

"Morning, Piper!" Emily replied, with some flakes of snow dropping onto her, "still freezing cold, isn't it?"

"I know!" she replied, "I just wish it was spring or summer now actually."

Emily loved the summer and everything about it where the trees would be nice and colorful, and the fish swimming freely without any evil creatures towards them, but couldn't, even Emily couldn't control winter as it was freezing and very crisp.

On Christmas Eve night, when all of the streets in the world were asleep and snow falling slowly than quickly as a flash, Emily took one last flight around the forest she had lived in and thought she was the only Christmas Kingfisher in the forest, but miraculously out of nowhere, a whole parade of Christmas Kingfishers came out and sang some carols and for Emily and her friend Piper, they joined in and the singing of this remarkable choir of festive kingfishers lasted until the sun had rose the following morning, where after little children viciously unwrapped their gifts and couldn't hardly wait for the next Christmas to come.

Tale 4:

The Best Christmas Gift

Now everything had been decorated just in time for the Christmas holidays, and some of Gortmill, the place where we set our story, was covered in blankets of snow. Thick blankets they were – not too high, nor an inch and the Christmas lights that were put on every single tree in every single house in the city, shone a luminous light that even the people who lived outside of the city could see it, and thought it was unregretful to see.

Hatty McDonald had just gone outside where cars were coming up and down the street she lived in and walked to the pond, where it had a green-coated wooden fence surrounding it, where the water was all polar and icy, which had made her think, "What would happen to the goldfish if the pond was numb and antarctic, not be able to break?"

As matter of fact, Hatty loved nature and the environment. She was also a bookworm and in the corner of her room, all decorated in all types of different themes, there were two bookshelves completely full of books, from the classic children books to picture books either written by *Dr. Seuss* or the funny, comedic books by *Michael Rosen* and *David Walliams*, and loved watching BBC documentaries about wildlife, especially loved watching *David Attenborough* as well, who is a famous naturalist in plants and animals.

"Good morning Hatty!" a man said, who surprised her that made her jump, "I see that you are curious about nature again at this wonderful time of year, am I wrong?"

The man was indeed a postman who had known Hatty since she was a baby. He had coal-black hair, and his skin was delicate as a pearl's surface and eyes that shone the light of day. His eyes were brown, but in the right corner, just near amongst the bone to the eye-socket and the skin that were next to his nose, there was a nip of dark yellow that made him kind and not selfish and would have time possible to help and talk, even if his and Hatty's conversation lasted until three or four in the afternoon, he loved to communicate with others, no matter of their height.

"Yes, Sam!" Hatty replied, giving him a smile back. "I am just wondering if fish can live through these cold conditions."

"Have you asked Father Christmas for that *Encyclopedia of Nature* yet in your wish list to him?"

Hatty shook her head, and got up and walked towards him. "Probably he is too busy with everyone else's presents that he won't have time to be busy with me, so there is no point."

This proved his point. Sam the Postman didn't like when people were sad, especially when it came to people who he dearly cared about and by the look on Hatty's face, he sat next to her and got a piece of paper and a pen, and she looked down at the blank page, where it had been rested onto the top of a wooden plank and began to write. She started the letter with the words: "*Dear Father Christmas...*" and her handwriting was very neat and beautiful, just like her mum's, nor like her father's.

Later that night, just days before it was Christmas Day, Hatty sat at the dinner table, focusing her eyes on the piece of paper and still continued what to ask Father Christmas, thinking very attentively, with the smell of soup to lose her focus and finished it after spending countless hours writing and re-writing it.

"Have you now finished your wish list to Father Christmas?" Hatty's mum had asked.

"Yes, mummy!" Hatty replied, licking the blue envelope that was near the endless pages of the wish list, with writing Father Christmas' address on and putting a stamp on it as well, "now I can eat my supper."

On Christmas morning a few days later, just even before Sam's rounds had begun, where the robins would wake from their winter night's sleep and would sing their song tenderly and softly, with pitch so calm, Hatty went outside and on the doorstep, there was a wrapped-gift and she picked it up, closed the door, and went to the sofa where her mum was, opened it and was breath taken as it was a book about nature that she wanted (as I thought it waited to be a surprise) and hugged her mum. In her mum's ears, she whispered: "Merry Christmas, mummy."

Tale 5:

The Handmade Christmas Ornament

The morning sky was grey and white; and the fog had rolled in. It was also cold as it was a few days until it was Christmas and most of the villagers who lived in the little, peaceful town, *Peterson,* were awfully busy to get gifts and wrap them before the morning of Christmas came. Little children were excited as well as they were looking forward to speak to Santa to see what they wanted for Christmas – even if it was a few days away.

Meryl was awoken to the sound of tapping by the winter-robins on the crisscrossed windows, but once one tap was made, as she tried to ignore it and the mouth-watering smell that led to the serving-counter in the kitchen, another tap was made and decided to give in and get up. She got out of bed, put her pink dressing-gown on and white slippers, which were satiny and fluffy, opened her bedroom door and closed it with only a notch of it open and walked downstairs to the kitchen where her mum was.

"Morning, Meryl," her Mum said, "did you enjoy your sleep after having that shocking headache you had from the heat of the fire?"

The night before, Meryl had a massive headache that made her faint, and then be unwell and almost been sick to one's stomach and almost called Dr. Smell, who smelled of raw fish and garlic, that would make her all green and retch.

"I am going to Granny Maud's later, Mum," Meryl announced, giving her a reply. "Is that alright?"

Her mum nodded, slightly agreeing with her question, and had breakfast. The smell was microwaved croissants and a hot chocolate; and as she ate it, her throat was piquant and shed happy tears as well. She loved it. Time had now passed and she was now dressed and headed out, to her Granny's cottage, that were not far from where she had lived.

She closed the gate and went walking. Walking down the back way of the church, walking past the Pub, walking past the Cinema where best friends would meet, all the way down Main Street to get to the cottage. Granny Maud's cottage had a name, and was called, *Elpfenn Place*. The bricks were practically all new, and even though the cottage was a hundred and so years old, when visitors would visit, they would think that it had just been built, but if you ask Granny Maud, who is a polite, frail little thing, she would say: "It looks new because it has just been furnished, and it is over a century old."

Meryl opened the front door of the cottage and closed it. She made sure that her Granny wouldn't hear her and wanted it to be a surprise, kind of sweet really.

"Meryl, darling," the croaky voice of Granny Maud asked, "is that you who has just walked in?"

She walked down the little hallway that was either side the stairs and the corridor was narrow and when guests would come in, they would feel a bone-chilling tickle down their spine and make up ridiculous stories about it been haunted.

"Yes, it is Granny Maud." Meryl replied.

Meryl came through the door and gave her a smile, a smile that was so small, it actually made Granny Maud laugh.

"My favorite granddaughter!" the old woman cried, stretching her arms out, "give Granny Maud a kissy."

She walked to her, gave her a kiss, and sat down.

"How is your mother?" Granny Maud asked, giving Meryl a great wide smile.

"Yes, Granny Maud," Meryl replied, with the sweetest sort of voice she had expressed as her vocal cords were less croaky than her Gran's when she was younger.

By the time she had left, it had now become night and snow was falling fast, just as fast as a flash as she ran through the narrow, steep road of the Main Street and hurried through the gate, closed it, opened the door and shut it so her mother wouldn't get fears that it was a burgular trying to steal, and went to bed, walking up the stairs; with the classic move of the tip-toes.

When it finally reached Christmas morning, Meryl ran straight downstairs, with her mother behind her, and opened the mountain of 99 presents, and one of them was a handmade Christmas ornament that reminded her of what she used to get on her first ever Christmas, over ten Christmas' ago.

Tale 6:

A Christmas in The Landscapes

By the time Crystal had finished her letter to her best friend Sophie, who lived in America, she put her pen away and put the neat-handwritten letter in the envelope.

"Have you finished your letter to Maud?" Crystal's mother tenderly, and politely said to her.

Crystal had nodded and put the letter into the envelope – that was indeed a blue envelope – and in the little town they lived in, blue envelopes were the mains of the post office that was down near the reservoir.

"Should I go to the post office now?" Crystal asked, letting off a yawn.

"I think you should," her mother replied, "it is nearly time for the Postman to come and take the mail away. So you best run."

Crystal really didn't want to do it, but if she walked slowly, it wouldn't arrive in time for Christmas, so she put her coat and shoes on, and ran down the village streets to the postbox and by the time she put the envelope in, the Postman had arrived.

"I see you got a letter for your American friend, Sophie?" the Postman said, just been nosy as usual.

Crystal nodded and left. She ran back home, and as she walked through the gate, the sunset had just gone and the ball of silver had came – that moon! That majestic moon.

"Did you run into the Postman?" Crystal's mother said.

"Yes!" she barked, "and that Postman is very nosy."

"Well, at least Christmas is tomorrow and then after the holidays, we can visit Sophie, like a catch-up."

Crystal was delighted. Of course she would be delighted, and saw that visiting her friend in January would be the best Christmas present soon to be unwrapped.

Tale 7:

The Dressmaker's Wonderful Idea

"What dress should I make Lord Winslow's daughter for the gala on Christmas Eve?" the Dressmaker thought to himself, whilst he was sat at his desk one day in his little workshop.

The cold, chilly weather in mid-December made the Dressmaker's hands numb and hopeless as the cold settled in more and whilst he was not working, he would love to write poems and stories for children and lived in the house where Lord and Lady Winslow had lived, along with their maids and butlers, and their only child – a daughter called Amelia.

One day, as the day was still cold, when the Dressmaker was in his little workshop working very hard on the dress that Lord Winslow instructed him to do, the Lord's daughter, Lorraine, had walked in the workshop.

"Hello, Miss Lorraine," the dressmaker had said to the girl who had plaits of midnight-blue hair, "how are you today?"

"Yes, I am great and it's not long until the Christmas Eve gala, is it Miss?"

The Dressmaker zipped up the dress in a glossy zip-bag and put it in the back of the workshop and locked the door. He and Lorraine went out, and took a long, relaxing walk across the magnificent gigantic gardens of where the Winslow's manor was.

Then as he walked back, he had an amazing idea and that was too make a better dress for her with some expensive fabrics and made it in time for the gala on Christmas Eve, which had gone pretty well and the holidays went well as well.